A MISSION FOR THE PEOPLE:
The Story of La Purisima

•••

Mary Ann Fraser

Henry Holt and Company ◆ New York

For Marc Aronson

Henry Holt and Company, Inc., *Publishers since 1866*
115 West 18th Street, New York, New York 10011

Henry Holt is a registered
trademark of Henry Holt and Company, Inc.

Published in Canada by Fitzhenry & Whiteside Ltd.,
195 Allstate Parkway, Markham, Ontario L3R 4T8.

Library of Congress Cataloging-in-Publication Data
Fraser, Mary Ann.
A mission for the people: the story of La Purisima /
Mary Ann Fraser.
Includes bibliographical references.
1. Chumash Indians—Missions—Juvenile literature.
Mission La Purisima Concepción (Calif.)—Juvenile
literature. I. Title.
E99.C815F73 1997 979.4'0049757—dc21 97-2692
ISBN 0-8050-5050-7 / First Edition—1997
The artist used acrylic on Strathmore bristol
to create the illustrations for this book.
Printed in the United States of America
on acid-free paper.∞
10 9 8 7 6 5 4 3 2 1

Author's Note

Missions have been the meeting place for many peoples and cultures. Unfortunately, most of the people at these missions, including many soldiers and Native Americans, could not read or write. As a result we have little evidence of how they felt. Such is the case with Mission La Purisima. Nearly all early historical accounts of the mission were written from a religious or Spanish point of view, while the voice of the soldiers and the Chumash went unrecorded. In writing this book, I have tried to take into account all points of view while remembering that there are always many ways to interpret history.

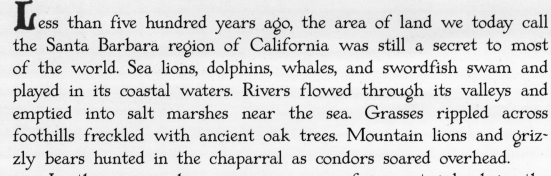

A Land of Riches

Less than five hundred years ago, the area of land we today call the Santa Barbara region of California was still a secret to most of the world. Sea lions, dolphins, whales, and swordfish swam and played in its coastal waters. Rivers flowed through its valleys and emptied into salt marshes near the sea. Grasses rippled across foothills freckled with ancient oak trees. Mountain lions and grizzly bears hunted in the chaparral as condors soared overhead.

In the warm, dry summers, ocean fog crept inland in the evenings and retreated in the late morning. During the cool, wet winters the brown hills turned to brilliant green.

The land was rich in resources and offered much to the people who lived on it. These people called themselves the Chumash. Their ancestors came to the region during the Ice Age, following herds of prehistoric bison and elk. As the climate warmed, the land changed, making it easy for the Chumash to hunt animals and to gather plants for food. The sea and land provided them with everything they needed. Their religious beliefs, music, and ceremonies celebrated the natural world that gave them so much.

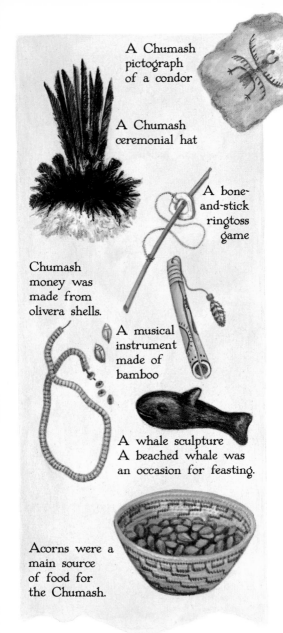

A Chumash pictograph of a condor

A Chumash ceremonial hat

A bone-and-stick ringtoss game

Chumash money was made from olivera shells.

A musical instrument made of bamboo

A whale sculpture
A beached whale was an occasion for feasting.

Acorns were a main source of food for the Chumash.

The First People

Since the weather was mild, the Chumash did not need much clothing. Women wore deerskin or rabbit-skin skirts decorated with shells and other ornaments. The men wore only a hide or fiber loincloth. Body paint and jewelry added the finishing touches.

The Chumash made many useful and beautiful things out of shell, bone, wood, stone, and plants. When they needed other materials from outside their homeland, they could easily trade for them. Young and old lived together in dome-shaped homes called *aps,* which were built of willow poles and thatched reeds. Their greatest achievement was the *tomol,* or planked canoe. These swift-gliding boats made it possible to fish and to travel between the mainland and the nearby Channel Islands.

For thousands of years the Chumash enjoyed the fruits of their land. Then on October 10, 1542, Juan Cabrillo, a Portuguese explorer working for Spain, sailed into the channel. This first encounter, although uneventful, was the start of drastic changes for the Chumash and their land.

In 1542 the Chumash called this site Algsacupi.

A coastal Chumash village, October 1542

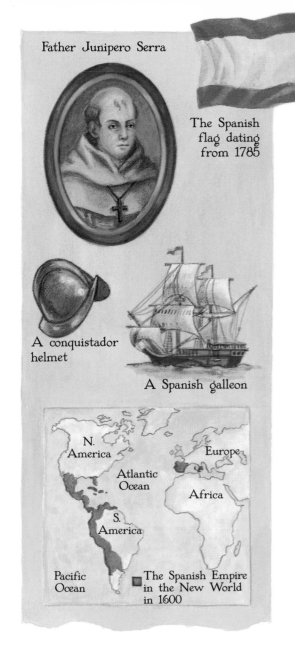

Father Junipero Serra

The Spanish flag dating from 1785

A conquistador helmet

A Spanish galleon

N. America

Europe

Atlantic Ocean

Africa

S. America

Pacific Ocean

The Spanish Empire in the New World in 1600

A Struggling Empire Claims California

Wars over religion had a long history in Spain. The year Columbus arrived in the New World, Spanish Catholics won their five hundred year struggle to drive Muslims and Jews out of the country. Wherever Spanish explorers journeyed, they claimed the land and its riches and converted the people to Christianity.

In 1512, Spanish conquistadores arrived in New Spain, which is today's Mexico. Soon New Spain became the centerpiece of Spain's mighty empire in the West. From there, Spanish galleons could easily sail across the Pacific Ocean to Asia to trade for silk, jewels, gold, and other treasures.

By the late eighteenth century the British and the Russians began sending expeditions to upper, or *alta,* California. Spain had to act quickly to protect its trade interests and colonies to the south. The Spanish thought that building missions and *presidios* (forts) in upper California would do the job. Their idea was that missionaries would teach the native people, or "Indians" as the Spanish called them, about the Christian God and European ways. The converted Indians would then become Spanish citizens. The soldiers would defend Spain's claim to the land and protect the missionaries from other Indians and Europeans.

A very religious and dedicated man named Father Junipero Serra was chosen by Spain to help build the first settlement in Alta California. Serra was enthusiastic about the job. All his life he had dreamed of spreading the Christian message. Sadly, over half of Serra's expedition members died during their journey to California. Still, he managed to found the first mission in San Diego in 1769. He saw it as the first link in a chain of missions dotting the coast of California. Father Serra lived to construct only nine missions. After Serra's death in 1784, Father Lasuén took up Serra's work.

Spanish soldiers and padres arrive in California to found a new mission in March 1787.

A mission hymnal

The Chumash valued the beads and metal objects the padres gave to them.

* Chumash village
† La Purisima

Santa Barbara Channel

Pacific Ocean

Channel Islands

Birth of a Mission

On December 8, 1787, the Spanish began a new mission in the land of the Chumash. With the sprinkling of holy water and the erection of a large wooden cross, Father Lasuén founded Mission La Purisima Concepción de Maria Santisima. It was Spain's eleventh mission in Alta California.

For Mission La Purisima to survive, the *padres*, or fathers, needed a church and shelters, their own food supply, and tools. That meant they needed converts; they needed the Chumash.

Most of the Chumash ignored the Spaniards. But a few admired the padres' gifts of clothing and trinkets, the soldiers' metal tools and guns, and the strange new European music. These people became the missionaries' first followers.

Mission La Purisima Concepción de Maria Santisima, Algsacupi, 1789

Baptizing the first Chumash converts, 1788

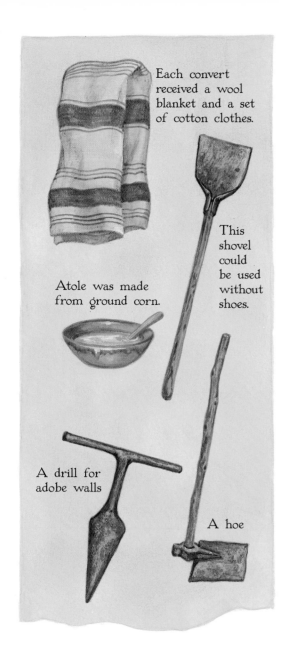

Each convert received a wool blanket and a set of cotton clothes.

Atole was made from ground corn.

This shovel could be used without shoes.

A drill for adobe walls

A hoe

The Chumash Learn Spanish Ways

The missionaries taught the converts about Christianity, baptized them, and brought them to live at the mission. Although the padres learned some of the Chumash language, they preferred to teach the Chumash to speak Spanish. If the converts tried to run away, the soldiers hunted them down and dragged them back.

The Chumash paid more attention to nature than to schedules. The sun and seasons were their clocks and calendars. But the missionaries believed a life of strict discipline was good for the soul. Days at the mission followed a rigid schedule. Bells tolled each morning to announce the beginning of the day and mass. While the adults went to work, the children stayed behind for religious education. After the midday meal and a rest period called a *siesta*, the Chumash worked for a few more hours. Then the bells tolled once again for the evening meal and prayers.

The converts wore woolen garments of European design that were woven in the mission's workshops. And instead of acorns and many other kinds of native plants and game, they ate mostly *atole*, a cornmeal soup, and *pozole*, a meat and vegetable stew. Only during certain months did the padres permit the Chumash to return to their villages to hunt and gather.

In Spain and Mexico men and women slept and ate separately. The padres insisted on these same rules for the Chumash at the mission. They divided families, sending the young women to live in a *monjerio*, or girls' dormitory. The boys and single men slept in the corridors of the mission, and married couples lived in a nearby *rancheria*, or village.

Bells announce the midday meal, 1798

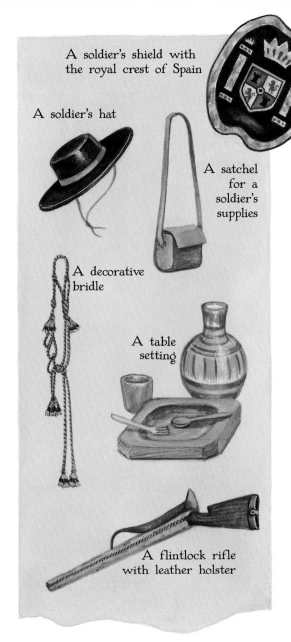

A soldier's shield with the royal crest of Spain

A soldier's hat

A satchel for a soldier's supplies

A decorative bridle

A table setting

A flintlock rifle with leather holster

The Military Master

While the soldiers were at the mission to defend Spain's claim to California, they also made sure the Chumash followed the king's rules.

For most soldiers in Alta California, being at the mission was a job and a chance to get some land of their own at the end of their duty. The five soldiers and one corporal assigned to each mission came from many different ethnic backgrounds. There were Spaniards, Africans, Mexican-Indians, and others, but all were Catholics.

Many soldiers had left their families and friends in other countries. Since Spanish and Mexican women often refused to travel to desolate Alta California, soldiers often married Chumash women. Unlike the Puritans of the Plymouth Plantation, Spain encouraged its citizens to marry native people.

The mission actually had two masters, soldiers and priests. While the military protected Spain's political interests, the clergy ran its religious matters. But these two purposes often led to conflict.

A disagreement between a soldier and a padre, 1800

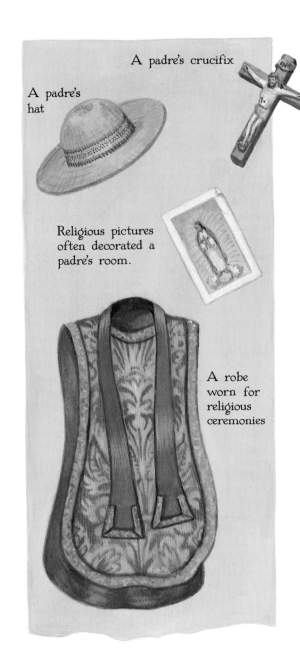

A padre's crucifix

A padre's hat

Religious pictures often decorated a padre's room.

A robe worn for religious ceremonies

The Religious Master

The Spanish missionaries were not interested in land or riches. They believed they were called by God to convert others to Christianity. They would endure anything to fulfill this task.

Usually two padres lived at La Purisima, sharing the many responsibilities of running the mission. While these men tended to be wise in the teachings of the church, they were often inexperienced in construction and agriculture.

By 1804 Mission La Purisima included over 1,500 Chumash converts, or "neophytes" as the Spanish called them. Adobe buildings surrounding a square replaced the original stick and mud structures.

In this same year Father Mariano Payeras arrived. His rare combination of kindness, enthusiasm, and business know-how began a period of prosperity for La Purisima.

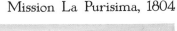

Mission La Purisima, 1804

Father Payeras visits the weavers, 1805

A Mexican chandelier

A gilded mirror from New England

A holy water vessel from Mexico

A cup and saucer from England

A teapot from China

A stretched cowhide to be traded by the mission for foreign goods

A Way of Life Disappears

Master artisans hired by the missionaries taught the Chumash European building techniques, farming methods, and animal husbandry. Nearly half of those who learned a trade left to work on the fifty or so ranches that supported the mission. The workers' small wages were later collected by the padres to support the entire mission community.

As more and more outside traders came to California's central coast, life outside the mission grew more difficult for the Chumash who had not converted. Russian, American, and Aleutian hunters drove the Chumash from their homes. These same foreign hunters also wiped out all of the sea otters, which were an important resource to the native people. Spanish *ranchos*, or ranches, took land away from the Chumash villages. Cattle trampled the water holes and grazed on useful native plants. Over time nearly all the Chumash came to live at the missions, adopt Spanish customs, and, in the process, to lose their traditional way of life.

Foreigners also brought their diseases. The Chumash had no resistance to these new viruses. Between 1804 and 1807 one of every three Chumash living at La Purisima died from smallpox, measles, or some other imported disease.

Father Payeras did his best to rally the survivors. While being part of the mission was hard for the Chumash, they shared the work, joined in the religious services, and built a life together.

Loading hides and tallow in a *carreta*, or cart, 1807

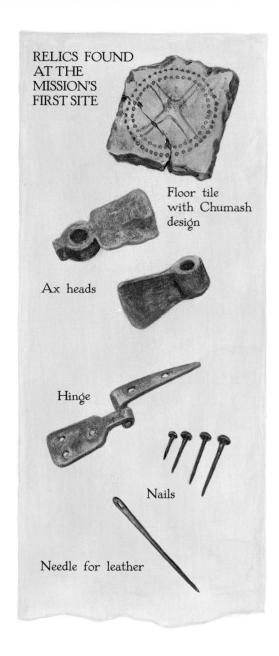

RELICS FOUND AT THE MISSION'S FIRST SITE

Floor tile with Chumash design

Ax heads

Hinge

Nails

Needle for leather

Disaster

On December 8, 1812, a series of tremors rocked La Purisima and much of California. Nerves were shaken, but little harm was done. Then, on December 21 at 10:30 A.M., a violent earthquake struck. The severe jolting toppled walls, sent plaster flying, and threw people to the ground. Dust choked the air.

Father Payeras and others rushed to help the injured and to check for damage. Suddenly a powerful aftershock hit, leveling the church and most of the other buildings.

Heavy rains followed. The broken adobe dissolved into mud and rubble. Only the domed huts of the Chumash remained intact.

Nature then delivered its final blow. The hillside backing the mission split open like a ripped seam and gushed forth a flood upon the site.

Some Chumash saw these events as a warning from Chupu, their ancient god. But the padres convinced most to stay at the mission. Everyone courageously worked together to find shelter, food, and clothes until the mission could be rebuilt.

Mission La Purisima, 1812

The earthquake, December 21, 1812, at 10:30 A.M.

Adobe brick

Adobe brick mold

Roof tiles, or *tejas*, were made on a wooden mold.

A clay water pipe

A floor tile, or *ladrillo*, with paw print. Dogs were sometimes used to guard drying tiles.

A -Cemetery
B -Bell tower
C -Church
D -Soap vats
E -Tallow vats
F -Mayordomo and soldiers' quarters, *carpenteria* (wood shop), and weavery
G -Padres' quarters
H -Pottery
I -*Pozalera*, or kitchen
J -Indian cemetery
K -Monjerio, or girls' dormitory
L -Indian residence building
M -*Lavanderias*, or wash basins
N -Blacksmith shop

A Time to Rebuild

When it came time to rebuild, Father Payeras chose a new site across the valley. The new mission had a better source of water, richer soil, and straddled El Camino Real (the Royal Road), which linked the Spanish missions.

In 1815 Father Payeras became *presidente*, or religious leader, of all the California missions. Most presidentes had lived at Mission San Carlos Borromeo in Carmel. Father Payeras chose to stay at La Purisima, making it the center of mission government.

Soon a new living area, two infirmaries for the sick, and a new church were nestled near the Purisima hills. Aqueducts, clay pipes, reservoirs, and dams brought water from six miles away.

Though the new mission was strong and well built, it was doomed. Once the British colonists in North America declared their independence in 1776, people throughout the Americas began to fight against their European masters. As Spain tried to keep control of New Spain, it found it could no longer afford to support the missions and presidios of California.

The Spanish called this new mission site Los Berros, 1821

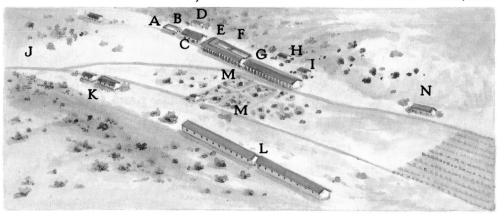

Building the new residence building, 1814

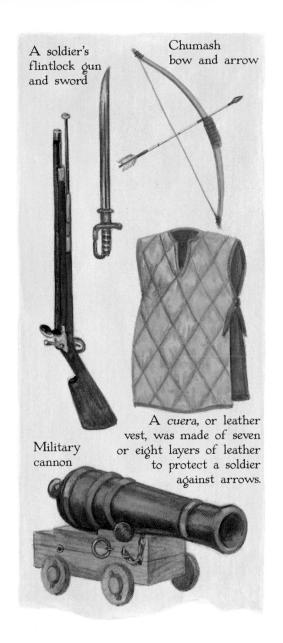

A soldier's flintlock gun and sword

Chumash bow and arrow

A *cuera*, or leather vest, was made of seven or eight layers of leather to protect a soldier against arrows.

Military cannon

A Time of Conflict and Revolt

In 1821 the citizens of New Spain won their independence from Spain. They named their new country Mexico. The Catholic church still controlled the missions, but Mexico now governed California.

The soldiers in the missions were now cut loose from Spain. More and more of them then used the Chumash converts for their own gain. Often the Indians were overworked or given harsh punishments, and the padres could do little to stop the abuse.

On April 29, 1823, worn out from his many responsibilities, the beloved Father Payeras died. To honor his great contribution to La Purisima, he was buried beneath the church's altar.

Without Father Payeras, tensions between the Chumash and the soldiers grew. On February 11, 1824, soldiers at Mission Santa Ines flogged a Purisima neophyte. When word reached La Purisima, the Chumash there revolted and seized control of the mission. When the governor sent a hundred soldiers from the Monterey presidio to La Purisima in mid-March, the Chumash were forced to surrender.

During the uprising some Chumash escaped from the mission. But they found they could not return to their traditional way of life. For most, the mission was the only home they had ever known. Eventually most of the runaways returned to La Purisima.

Spanish soldiers fire on Chumash rebels, March 19, 1824, at 8 A.M.

The Mexican flag of 1821

The lariat was the vaqueros' most useful tool.

A Mexican felt hat

Lady's hair combs

The Mexican colonists used clay to make many useful items.

Louisiana Purchase

Atlantic Ocean

Former Mexican territory

A Mexican California

Following the Mexican War of Independence in 1821 hundreds of settlers from Mexico flocked to upper California to claim land for themselves. People on the east coast of North America had combined European, African, and Native American customs. In a similar way the Mexicans had created a culture of their own—a rich blend of Spanish and native religions, languages, and customs—which they brought to California.

Many of these settlers earned a living raising livestock. The Mexicans were famous for their horsemanship. The *vaqueros* (horsemen) sometimes held rodeos to demonstrate their skills. Perched in finely tooled saddles, dressed in britches buttoned from hip to ankle, low boots, short jackets, and wide-brimmed felt hats, they would twirl their lariats and demonstrate their riding talents.

The women dressed modestly, with nothing left uncovered but their hands and faces. They wore dresses, kerchiefs to cover their necks and chests, stockings, and homemade shoes called *berruchis*. Their hair was piled up and held in place with small combs.

The Mexicans were Catholics, and they respected the padres of the missions, but raising livestock required many acres of grazing land. When the Mexican colonists realized the missions owned most of the good land, they became angry. They wondered why the church needed so much property. They argued that it should be in the hands of Mexican citizens.

A Mexican rodeo, 1826

CALIFORNIA MISSIONS

- - - - - El Camino Real
——— Connecting route

Sonoma, 1828

San Rafael, 1817

Dolores, 1776
Santa Clara, 1777
San Jose, 1797
Santa Cruz, 1791
San Juan Bautista, 1797

Carmel, 1770

Soledad, 1791

San Antonio, 1771

San Miguel, 1797

San Luis Obispo, 1772
La Purisima,
1787
Santa Ines, 1804

Santa Barbara,
1786
San
San Buenaventura, 1782
Fernando,
San Gabriel, 1771
1797

San Juan Capistrano, 1776

San Luis Rey, 1798

San Diego, 1769

The Mission in Private Hands

In 1833 the Mexican government snatched control of mission lands from the Catholic church.

The padres at La Purisima moved to Mission Santa Ines. The *Mayordomos* (ranch supervisors) assigned to each mission were to give the few surviving Chumash their shares of land, but these men were not always honest.

Within a short time most of the Chumash who received land abandoned it. The plots were too small to make a living, and the Mexican government forbade them to sell it.

The Chumash could not go back to their ancestral villages or hunting and gathering grounds. These areas now belonged to others. Some Chumash moved inland to live with other native Californians. Most went to work for the ranchos. Mexican settlers welcomed this cheap source of labor and created ways to keep their Chumash workers from leaving. The Chumash had lost what little protection the mission used to provide.

Mission La Purisima, 1856

A Chumash family leaves their land, 1886

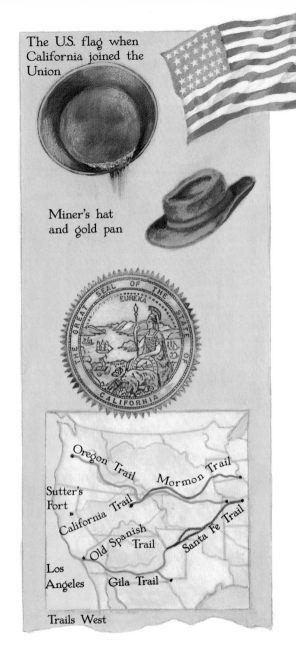

The U.S. flag when California joined the Union

Miner's hat and gold pan

Trails West

The Anglos Are Coming!

Many Americans believed it was the country's *manifest destiny,* or fate, for its citizens to settle land from the Atlantic coastline to the Pacific shores. California's resources and valuable ports made it especially attractive. In 1846 the United States declared war and invaded Mexico. Two years later the Treaty of Guadalupe Hidalgo ended the Mexican-American War. California, Texas, and New Mexico now belonged to the United States.

In January 1848, just a few miles beyond the most northern mission, a man named James Marshall discovered gold. The news spread quickly, and people from around the world poured into California. When the gold began to run out, miners stayed to build their own farms, ranches, and towns. So many Americans came to live in California that it was declared a state in 1850. By then only a few hundred Chumash remained of the ten thousand or so who had once lived in California. One year later, the United States returned La Purisima's church and other buildings to the Catholic church.

By far the largest group of these incoming Americans were the *Anglos,* people of European descent. Like each wave of immigrants before them, they wanted control of the land and its resources.

Meanwhile, La Purisima passed from owner to owner. Vandals carried away tiles to use elsewhere, winter rains dissolved the four-foot-thick walls, and drifting sand and silt blanketed the crumbling heaps of adobe. For over one hundred years thousands of people had lived and died rebuilding La Purisima. By the late 1920s it sat in ruin.

The monastery stands in ruin, 1930

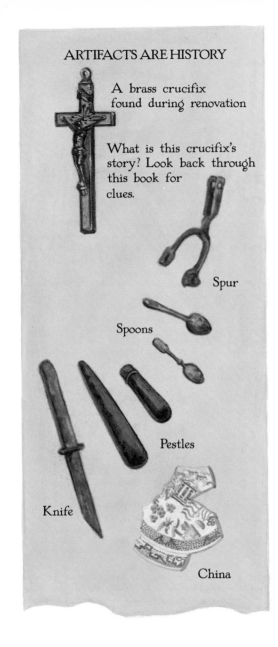

A brass crucifix found during renovation

What is this crucifix's story? Look back through this book for clues.

Spur

Spoons

Pestles

Knife

China

A Mission to Be Remembered

In 1933, during the Great Depression, the federal government created the Civilian Conservation Corps to put unemployed men back to work. A year later the corps began restoration on what was to become La Purisima Mission State Historical Monument. It is now the most completely restored of all the missions.

But the land and animals that once lived in the area could not be restored. Gone, too, are the full-blooded Chumash, but we remember their heritage as we travel their ancient hunting routes and adopt their place names. And their descendants continue to work to protect the environment throughout the world.

We remember the Spanish by the many products and processes they brought to the Western Hemisphere. Horses, cattle, sheep, and goats; irrigation methods and the plow; and fruit, nut, and citrus orchards are all from Spain. The Spanish language and architecture are present throughout the Southwest.

Descendants of those first Mexican settlers still live near La Purisima. While they are American citizens, they share their multiethnic heritage through their cooking, customs, and celebrations.

La Purisima today

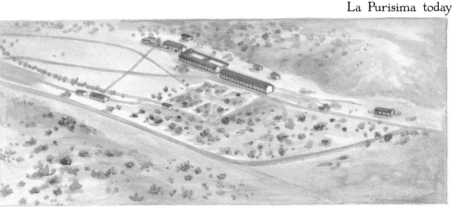

Renovation of the monastery, 1934

Our Cultural Inheritance

The Santa Barbara region and La Purisima represent much of what has happened during the settlement of the West. Like other parts of the country, people came to the area for many reasons. Some were in search of food, employment, land, or riches. Others wanted to spread their religion. All called it home.

Together these people of many nationalities helped build and preserve Mission La Purisima. While it may be little more than a cluster of buildings upon the land, it stands as a symbol. This, our inheritance, reminds us all that while the blending of peoples often brings conflict, it also enriches our lives.

Time Line

page numbers in parenthesis refer to text.

· SUGGESTED READING ·

Faber, Gail, and Michele Lasagna. *Whispers Along the Mission Trail.* Alamo, Calif.: Magpie, 1986.

Gibson, Robert O. *The Chumash.* New York: Chelsea House, 1991.

Krell, Dorothy. *The California Missions: A Pictorial History.* Menlo Park, Calif.: Sunset, 1979.

Kuska, George, and Barbara Linse. *Live Again: Our Mission Past.* Larkspur, Calif.: Arts' Books, 1983.

Neuerburg, Norman. *The Architecture of Mission La Purisima.* Santa Barbara, Calif.: Bellerophon Books, 1987.

Roberts, Helen M. *Mission Tales: Stories of the Historic California Missions.* Palo Alto, Calif.: Pacific Books, 1948.